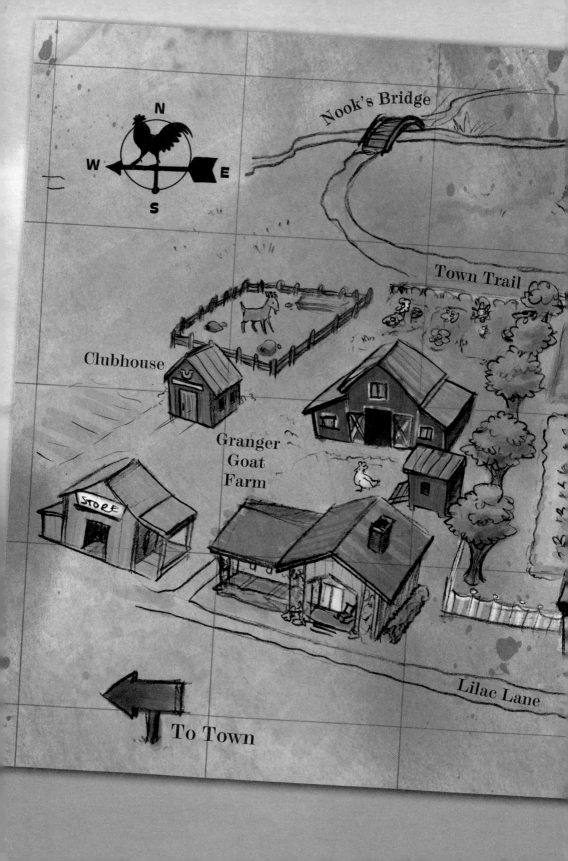

Pony MYSTERIES

THE Clue ·IN THE· Clubhouse

By Jeanne Betancourt

Illustrated by Kellee Riley

Cartwheel
B·O·O·K·S®

SCHOLASTIC INC.

New York   Toronto   London   Auckland

Sydney   Mexico City   New Delhi   Hong Kong

For Biulu, who loves a good story
at bedtime or anytime. — JB

Dedicated to my pony Spunky Pete, who
never would stop chasing butterflies. — KR

Text copyright © 2011 by Jeanne Betancourt.
Illustrations copyright © 2011 by Kellee Riley.

ISBN 978-0-545-11507-0

10 9 8 7 6 5 4 3 2 1   11 12 13 14 15

Printed in the U.S.A.   40
First edition, September 2011

Table of Contents

Chapter 1
A GREAT IDEA

My name is Penny Ryder.

I live in the city, but my grandma and grandpa live in the country.

I am living with them for the whole summer.

Last week I was a city kid with no pets.
Now I am a country kid with two pets.
I have a pony named Pepper and a kitten
named Lucky.

Tom and Tina Granger are my friends in
the country.
Tina, Tom, Pepper, and I are detectives.
We use clues to solve mysteries.

Lucky is not a detective. She is just an
adorable cat.

"What should we do today?" I ask my friends.

"Let's make a clubhouse," says Tina. "Mom said we can use our old shed."

"But we have to fix it up," adds Tom.
"It's a mess."

"Our clubhouse can be the office for our
detective agency," I say.
"That's a great idea," says Tina. "Let's
do it!"

Chapter 2
MY BIG SECRET

We open the gate and lead Pepper onto Town Trail. Town Trail goes from my house to Tom and Tina's goat farm.

"It's your turn to ride first, Penny," says Tina.

I don't want to ride. Riding scares me.

Tina and Tom don't know that I am afraid of riding.

"Hey," says Tom. "Look who wants to
come, too."
I turn around. Lucky is following us.

"I'll carry Lucky," I say. "You two ride Pepper."

Tom mounts Pepper and we follow the trail.

Pepper's ears twitch because
he's happy. He loves to go to the Granger
Goat Farm. I am happy, too—happy that
I don't have to ride.

When we get to the farm, I put Lucky down
and she runs into the barn.
"She'll be looking for mice," says Tom.
I wonder if she'll find any.

"Where's the clubhouse?" I ask.
Tom points to a red shed at the edge of
the field.

We run the whole way to the shed.
Pepper, too.

We spend all morning fixing up our clubhouse.

There are five empty wooden crates piled in a corner. Pepper discovers an old horseshoe under one of them.

We turn three of the crates over to use for chairs. We place the other two crates near the wall to make cubbies for our stuff.

We put the horseshoe over the front door for good luck.

"It is time for the first meeting in our clubhouse," says Tom.

I start the meeting with a question. "What do detectives need for solving mysteries?"

"We need a notebook for writing clues," says Tina.

"And a magnifying glass for finding them," adds Tom. "And snacks. We need snacks."

"And mystery books," I say. "Ones with detectives in them."

Chapter 3
PINK BALLET SLIPPER

We go into Tina and Tom's house for supplies.

Soon everything is put away in the cubbies.

"We need one more thing," I say. "We need a mystery to solve."

We sit on our crate chairs and read mystery books for ideas.

Someone knocks on our clubhouse door. It's Mrs. Granger. "This place looks great," she says. "Good job."
Tina and Tom's mom has the one thing that we are missing.

"I lost the key to my truck," she says. "But I don't have time to look for it. Can you help me?"

"You have come to the right place, Mom," says Tom. "We will find your key."

Tina opens her notebook. "First, we need clues," she says. "Can we ask you some questions?"

"Okay," says Mrs. Granger. "But in five minutes I have to open the store."
I ask the first question. "When did you last see this key, Mrs. Granger?"
"Six o'clock yesterday," she answers.
"That's when I came home in the truck."
Tina writes this first clue in our detective notebook.

"Where did you put the key?" Tina asks her mother.
"In my pocket," she says. "It must have fallen out." Tina writes some more.

"What did you do after you parked the truck?" asks Tom.

"I went to the barn to clean the goat pen," his mother answers.

"Which one?" asks Tina.

"The last one," she says, "near the back door."

Tom and I grin at each other. We have Clue #3.

"Don't worry, Mom," says Tom. "We'll find your key."

Mrs. Granger thanks us and goes to open the store.

"Come on, Pepper," I shout. "We have a mystery to solve."

"We should start our search at the truck," says Tina.

"And let's look between the truck and the barn," I say. "Maybe she dropped the key on the path."

We look inside the truck. Tom uses the magnifying glass.

No key.

Pepper finds an apple that rolled under the seat.

We search around the truck.

No key.

Next we walk slowly along the path between the truck and the barn.
No key.

The four of us go into the barn.

Tina looks through all the clean straw in the last stall.

Tom and I sweep the walkway that starts at the front door.

Still no key.

Keys, keys, keys, I think.

I feel in my pocket for my key to Grandma
and Grandpa's house. It is on a key ring
with a tiny, sparkly ballet slipper.

Chapter 4
MORE CLUES

"Is your mother's key on a key ring?" I ask Tom and Tina.

"I don't remember," says Tina.

"Me neither," says Tom. "Let's find out."

We run to the farm store. Pepper does not go with us. He wants to eat grass. We will have to solve this mystery without him.

Mrs. Granger is helping a customer. She looks over at us. "Did you find my key?" she asks.

"Not yet, Mom," says Tom.

She looks disappointed.

"Don't worry, Mrs. Granger," I say. "We will find your key. We just need more clues."

"Mom, is your key on a key chain?" asks Tina.

"Why, yes it is," she answers. "I should have told you that. My key is on my toy mouse key chain."

"A mouse key chain," says Tina. "That is Clue #4." She writes it in her notebook.

Mrs. Granger hands a customer his change. Good detectives notice everything. I notice that the customer is buying goat cheese and a jar of honey. The jar of honey is in a box with straw. The straw gives me an idea for a clue.

"Mrs. Granger, you said that you cleaned the pen," I say. "Where did you put the old straw?"

"I left it in the wheelbarrow," answers Mrs. Granger. "I didn't have time to empty it."

We run back to the barn.

We look through the old straw in the wheelbarrow.
No mouse key chain.
No key.

"We have found plenty of clues," I say.
"But we haven't solved the mystery of the missing key," says Tina.

"Something else is missing," says Tom.
"Where is Pepper?"
"Why isn't he helping us?" asks Tina.
"He's eating grass near the clubhouse,"
I answer.
"Let's go back there, too," says Tom. "I need a snack."
"We can have another meeting about the missing key," I say.

Chapter 5
NOT A TOY

Pepper is not in the field near the clubhouse.
He is in the clubhouse.

Pepper is sniffing at something in the corner.
He looks up at us and snorts.
He wants us to see Lucky, sleeping in a
patch of sunlight.

"Pepper came in here to see Lucky,"
says Tom.
"That is so cute," says Tina.
A big idea pops into my head. A mouse key
chain looks like a cat toy.

I pick up Lucky and there it is—a mouse key chain with Mrs. Granger's key.

"Lucky found it," Tom says, "and brought it here."

Lucky snuggles in my arms and purrs. "Good job, Lucky," says Tina. "You found the key."

Pepper whinnies and flicks his ears. He knows that he's the one who found the key. Lucky was just playing with a toy.

"You are right, Pepper," I say. "You did find the key and you showed it to us."

"Good job, Pepper," say Tom and Tina at the same time.

We all run back to the store to give Mrs. Granger her key. Tom, Tina, Pepper, Lucky, and me.

"Great work, detectives," she says. "And just in time. I need the truck to deliver goat's milk to the general store. May I pay you in cookies?"

"Yes!" we agree. She gives us each a big oatmeal chocolate chip cookie from the store cookie jar.

We head back to the clubhouse.
"We solved a mystery today," says Tina.
"And we made our clubhouse," adds Tom.
I say, "Now all we need is a name for our clubhouse."

I look at the horseshoe over the door.
Tina and Tom look at it, too.
"We are the Horseshoe Detectives," I say.

"The Horseshoe Detectives," repeats Tina.
"Yes!" agrees Tom.

Pepper nickers and throws back his head.
He likes it, too.

We make a sign with our clubhouse name
and put it over the door.

It has been a good day for the Horseshoe
Detectives.